I0648544

Anonymous

Songs and Verses

Social and Scientific

Anonymous

Songs and Verses
Social and Scientific

ISBN/EAN: 9783744769235

Printed in Europe, USA, Canada, Australia, Japan

Cover: Foto ©Andreas Hilbeck / pixelio.de

More available books at **www.hansebooks.com**

SONGS AND VERSES

SOCIAL AND SCIENTIFIC

BY

AN OLD CONTRIBUTOR TO MAGA

WILLIAM BLACKWOOD AND SONS
EDINBURGH AND LONDON
MDCCCLXVIII

PREFACE.

A GREAT proportion of these pieces were originally published in 'Blackwood's Magazine:' some appeared in the 'Scotsman' Newspaper; and the rest were written for the amusement of a Scientific Club, or of a circle of private friends. They were received at the time with some approbation; and they are now collected mainly in the hope of preserving or reviving in the minds of those who were then pleased to approve of them a recollection of the feelings that attended their first reception.

CONTENTS.

SONGS AND VERSES,

SOCIAL AND SCIENTIFIC.

THE ORIGIN OF SPECIES.

A NEW SONG.

Have you heard of this question the Doctors among,
Whether all living things from a Monad have sprung?
This has lately been said, and it now shall be sung,
   Which nobody can deny.

Not one or two ages sufficed for the feat,
It required a few millions the change to complete;
But now the thing's done, and it looks rather neat,
   Which nobody can deny.

The original Monad, our great-great-grandsire,
To little or nothing at first did aspire;
But at last to have offspring it took a desire,
   Which nobody can deny.

This Monad becoming a father or mother,
By budding or bursting, produced such another;
And shortly there followed a sister or brother,
         Which nobody can deny.

But Monad no longer designates them well—
They're a cluster of molecules now, or a cell;
But which of the two, Doctors only can tell,
         Which nobody can deny.

These beings, increasing, grew buoyant with life,
And each to itself was both husband and wife;
And at first, strange to say, the two lived without strife,
         Which nobody can deny.

But such crowding together soon troublesome grew,
And they thought a division of labour would do;
So their sexual system was parted in two,
         Which nobody can deny.

Thus Plato supposes that, severed by fate,
Human halves run about, each in search of its mate,
Never pleased till they gain their original state,
         Which nobody can deny.

Excrescences fast were now trying to shoot;
Some put out a finger, some put out a foot;
Some set up a mouth, and some sent down a root,
         Which nobody can deny.

Some, wishing to walk, manufactured a limb ;
Some rigged out a fin, with a purpose to swim ;
Some opened an eye, some remained dark and dim,
          Which nobody can deny.

Some creatures grew bulky, while others were small,
As nature sent food for the few or for all ;
And the weakest, we know, ever go to the wall,
          Which nobody can deny.

A deer with a neck that was longer by half
Than the rest of its family's (try not to laugh),
By stretching and stretching, became a Giraffe,
          Which nobody can deny.

A very tall pig, with a very long nose,
Sends forth a proboscis quite down to his toes ;
And he then by the name of an Elephant goes,
          Which nobody can deny.

The four-footed beast that we now call a Whale,
Held its hind-legs so close that they grew to a tail,
Which it uses for threshing the sea like a flail,
          Which nobody can deny.

Pouters, tumblers, and fantails are from the same source ;
The racer and hack may be traced to one Horse :
So Men were developed from Monkeys, of course,
          Which nobody can deny.

An Ape with a pliable thumb and big brain,
When the gift of the gab he had managed to gain,
As a Lord of Creation established his reign,
         Which nobody can deny.

But I'm sadly afraid, if we do not take care,
A relapse to low life may our prospects impair;
So of beastly propensities let us beware,
         Which nobody can deny.

Their lofty position our children may lose,
And, reduced to all-fours, must then narrow their views;
Which would wholly unfit them for filling our shoes,
         Which nobody can deny.

Their vertebræ next might be taken away,
When they'd sink to an oyster, or insect, some day,
Or the pitiful part of a polypus play,
         Which nobody can deny.

Thus losing Humanity's nature and name,
And descending through varying stages of shame,
They'd return to the Monad, from which we all came,
         Which nobody can deny.

May 1861.

THE MEMORY OF MONBODDO.

AN EXCELLENT NEW SONG. .

Air—The Looking-Glass.

'TIS strange how men and things revive
 Though laid beneath the sod, O !
I sometimes think I see alive
 Our good old friend Monboddo !
His views, when forth at first they came,
 Appeared a little odd, O !
But now we've notions much the same ;
 We're back to old Monboddo.

The rise of Man he loved to trace
 Up to the very pod, O !
And in Baboons our parent race
 Was found by old Monboddo.
Their A B C he made them speak,
 And learn their *Qui, quæ, quod*, O !
Till Hebrew, Latin, Welsh, and Greek
 They knew as well's Monboddo.

The thought that Men had once had tails
  Caused many a grin full broad, O !
And why in us that feature fails,
  Was asked of old Monboddo.
He showed that sitting on the rump,
  While at our work we plod, O !
Would wear th' appendage to the stump
  As close as in Monboddo.

Alas ! the good lord little knew,
  As this strange ground he trod, O !
That others would his path pursue,
  And never name Monboddo !
Such folks should have their tails restored,
  And thereon feel the rod, O !
For having thus the fame ignored
  That's due to old Monboddo.

Though Darwin now proclaim the law,
  And spread it far abroad, O !
The man that first the secret saw,
  Was honest old Monboddo.
The Architect precedence takes
  Of him that bears the hod, O !
So up and at them, Land of Cakes !
  We'll vindicate Monboddo.

The Scotchman who would grudge his praise,
   Must be a senseless clod, O !
A MONUMENT then let us raise,
   To honour old Monboddo.
Let some great artist sketch the plan,
   While Rogers * gives the nod, O !
A Monkey changing to a Man !
   In memory of Monboddo.

* The Rev. promoter of the Wallace Monument.

September 1861.

THE DARWINIAN ERA OF FARMING.

Air—Derry Down.

O ! Farming's not merely an art of some skill ;
It's a Science, or something more excellent still :
For the Farmer has such a command over nature,
You almost might call him a kind of Creator :
     Singing down, down, down, derry down.

'Twas long ago found that a Horse and an Ass
Breed a good kind of beast for a mountainous pass ;
But since Mules were invented, it never till now
Was supposed you could breed from a Horse and a Cow :
     Singing down, down, down, derry down.

But all nowadays to their lessons must look :
So the Farmer must read Mr Darwin's great book,
Who proves or asserts, and has credit from some,
That from all sorts of creatures all others may come :
     Singing down, down, down, derry down.

If this theory holds and we find the right way,
There's no end of the freaks that the Farmer may play ;

Getting all sorts of products from all sorts of stocks,
He may ride on his Ram and clip wool from his Ox :
　　Singing down, down, down, derry down.

He may breed you a beast mingled just half and half,
From a fortunate cross of a Pig and a Calf;
When you'll cut without trouble, so neat and so nice,
Both your ham and your veal in the very same slice :
　　Singing down, down, down, derry down.

As now well established beyond any question,
Variety's good both for taste and digestion ;
And a Hybrid would prove a prodigious relief,
With the fore-quarter *mutton*, the hind-quarter *beef :*
　　Singing down, down, down, derry down.

You must never lose heart if your mules seldom breed,
Or if some of your mixtures at first don't succeed ;
Mr Darwin himself would exhort you to wait,
As he draws his own bills at a very long date :
　　Singing down, down, down, derry down.

So, perhaps, when their practical worth you explore,
There's not much in these notions we hadn't before ;
For they'll scarcely come true (what a subject for
　· laughter !)
Till the great day of Judgment,—or say the day After :
　　Singing down, down, down, derry down.

THE ORIGIN OF LANGUAGE.

AN EXCELLENT NEW SONG.

Air—Let Schoolmasters puzzle their brains.

'TIS not very easy to tell
　　How language had first a beginning,
When Adam had just left the shell,
　　And Eve hadn't taken to spinning ;
Or if, in some other queer way,
　　Men rose to be lords of creation,
What power brought their tongues into play,
　　Or prompted their speechification ?
　　　　　　Toroddle, toroddle, toroll.

Some think men were ready inspired
　　With lexicon, syntax, and grammar,
And never like children required
　　At lessons to lisp and to stammer.
As Pallas by Jove was begot
　　In armour all brilliantly burnished,
So Man with his Liddell and Scott
　　And old Lindley Murray was furnished.
　　　　　　Toroddle, toroddle, toroll.

Some say that the primitive tongue
 Expressed but the simplest affections;
And swear that the words said or sung
 Were nothing but mere Interjections.
O ! O ! was the signal of pain :
 Ha ! Ha ! was the symptom of laughter :
Pooh ! Pooh ! was the sign of disdain,
 And *Hillo !* came following after.
  Toroddle, toroddle, toroll.

Some, taking a different view,
 Maintain the old language was fitted
To mark out the objects we knew,
 By mimicking sounds they emitted.
Bow, wow was the name for a dog :
 Quack, quack was the word for a duckling :
Hunc, hunc would designate a hog,
 And *wee, wee* a pig and a suckling.
  Toroddle, toroddle, toroll.

Who knows if what Adam might speak,
 Was mono- or poly-syllabic ;
Was Gothic, or Gaelic, or Greek,
 Tartaric, Chinese, or Arabic.
It may have been Sanscrit or Zend —
 It must have been something or other ;

But thus far I'll stoutly contend,
  It wasn't the tongue of his mother.
        Toroddle, toroddle, toroll.

If asked these hard things to explain,
  I own I am wholly unable;
And hold the attempt the more vain,
  When I think of the building of Babel.
Then why should we puzzle our brains
  With Etymological clatter?
The prize wouldn't prove worth the pains,
  And the missing it isn't much matter.
        Toroddle, torrodle, toroll.

In courtship suppose you can't sing,
  Your Cara, your Liebe, your Zoe,
A kiss and a sight of the ring
  Will more quickly prevail with your Chloe.
Or if you in twenty strange tongues
  Could call for a beef-steak and bottle,
A purse with less learning and lungs,
  Would bring them much nearer your throttle.
        Toroddle, toroddle, toroll.

I've ranged, without drinking a drop,
  The realms of the dry Mithridates :
I've studied Grimm, Burnouf, and Bopp,
  Till patience cried " *Ohe jam satis.*"

Max Müller completed my plan,
  And, leave of the subject now taking,
As wise as when first I began,
  I end with a head that is aching.
            Toroddle, toroddle, toroll.

The speech of Old England for me ;
  It serves us on every occasion !
Henceforth, like our soil, let it be
  Exempted from foreign invasion.
It answers for friendship and love,
  For all sorts of feeling and thinking ;
And lastly, all doubt to remove—
  It answers for singing and drinking.
            Toroddle, toroddle, toroll.

February 1862.

GRIMM'S LAW.

A NEW SONG.

Air—Old Homer,—but with him what have we to do?

[In a late Number of the 'Anthropological Review' Grimm's law
is explained in what is at least an ingenious manner.   After describing an Aryan, or "articulate-speaking man," setting out to teach language to some rude owners of the "kitchen-middens" of the prim-
eval age, who are supposed to be speechless, a distinguished Anthro-
pologist thus reports the result of the attempt : "But now assume
the 200 [kitchen-middeners] to be mutes, and follow the leader of
the Aryans in his first lesson to the crowd around him.   Naturally
he would get the crowd to pronounce after him some short syllables,
such as *pa*, *ta*, *ka*, to illustrate the use of lips, palate, and throat,
and very naturally the four or five men (or women more likely) just
in front of him would pronounce them rightly, but not one man in
fifty can tell the real effect of his work on a crowd.   On their return-
ing to their wigwams much would be the emotion of risibility and
imitativeness displayed that night among the natives ; and next
morning the chances are that the majority who stood some distance
from the speaker would have fixed for ever upon the whole nation
the wrong utterance of *ba*, *da*, *ga*.   The main point of my whole
argument is, that such a result would most naturally follow among
mutes, but would never happen among speaking men."—*Extract
from Paper read before the Anthropological Society by the* Rev. D. I.
HEATH, M.A.—*Anthropological Review*, April 1867.]

ETYMOLOGY once was a wild kind of thing,
Which from any one word any other could bring :

Of the consonants then the effect was thought small,
And the vowels—the vowels were nothing at all.
>> Down a down, down, &c.

But that state of matters completely is changed,
And the old school of scholars now feels quite estranged :
For 'tis clear that whenever we open our jaw,
Every sound that we utter comes under some Law.

Now one of these laws has been named after Grimm,
For the Germans declare it was found out by him :
But their rivals the Danes take the Germans to task,
And proclaim as its finder the great Rasmus Rask.

Be this as it may, few have sought to explain
How it came that this law could its influence gain :
Max Müller has tried, and, perhaps, pretty well ;
But I don't understand him, and therefore can't tell.

Anthropologists say, after Man had his birth,
There were two human races possessing the earth ;
One gifted and graced with articulate speech,
And another that only could gabble and screech.

The Aryans could speak, and could build, and could
>> plough,
And knew most of the arts we are practising now ;
But the Dumbies that dwelt at those vile Kitchen-Middens
Weren't fit but to do their superiors' biddings.

So an Aryan went forth to enlighten these others,
And to raise them by speech to the level of brothers;
On the Mutes of the Middens he burst with éclat,
And attempted to teach them the syllable PA.

This PA was intended to set things a-going
For a lot of Good Words very well worth the knowing;
Such as Pater, and πολις, and Panis, and Pasco;
But the Midden performers made rather a *fiasco*.

Scarce one of them all would say PA for a wonder,
But each blundered away with a different blunder:
Some feebly cried A, and some, crow-like, said KA,
While the nearest they came to was FA or was BA.

Then the Aryan propounded the syllable TA,
Which his pupils corrupted to THA and to DA:
Even KA, when they tried it, they never came nearer
Than to HA or to GA, or to something still queerer.

So slow were their senses to seize what was said,
That they never could hit the right nail on the head;
And the game of cross purposes lasted so long,
That it soon was a rule they should always go wrong.

Thus the Dumbies for ever said Father for Pater,
And Bearing and Brother for Ferens and Frater:
The Aryan cried Pecu, the Midden-man Fee,
In which Doctors and Lawyers to this day agree.

Jove's Tonitru sank into Old Saxon Thunner,
Which the High-German dunderheads changed into
　　Donner;
From Domo came Tame, and from Domus came Timmer,
While the hissing Helvetians said Zämen and Zimmer.

From θυρα came Door, and from θυγατηρ Dochter,
Which dwindled away into Türe and Tochter:
From Hortus and Hostis came Garden and Guest,
And from χολη came Gall, which so bothers the best.

The Old Aryan GAU was the Kitchener's Koo
(Though some tribes were contented to call the beast
　　Boo):
If your wife in her καρδια would give you a Cornu,
The Midden-man said, " In her Heart she would Horn
　· you."

Such a roundabout race I can only compare
To the whirligig engines we mount at a fair;
Where each rides as in fear lest his steed be forsaken,
But he ne'er overtakes, and is ne'er overtaken.

A theory seldom is free from a flaw,
But the story I've told may account for Grimm's law:
Though some others suggest, if the Bible's no fable,
That Grimm's law was what caused the confusion at Babel.
　　　　　Down a down, down, &c.

December 1867.

STUART MILL ON MIND AND MATTER.*

A NEW SONG.

Air—Roy's wife of Aldivalloch.

Stuart Mill, on Mind and Matter,
All our old Beliefs would scatter :
Stuart Mill exerts his skill
To make an end of Mind and Matter.

The self-same tale I've surely heard,
    Employed before, our faith to batter :
Has David Hume again appeared,
    To run a-muck at Mind and Matter?

David Hume could Mind and Matter
Ruthlessly assault and batter :
Those who Hume would now exhume
Must mean to end both Mind and Matter.

---

* " Matter, then, may be defined a Permanent Possibility of Sensation."—*Mill's Examination of Hamilton*, p. 198.

" The belief I entertain that my mind exists, when it is not feeling, nor thinking, nor conscious of its own existence, resolves itself into the belief of a Permanent Possibility of these states." " The Permanent Possibility of feeling, which forms my notion of Myself."
—*Ibid.*, p. 205, 206.

Now Mind, now Matter, to destroy,
    Was oft proposed, at least the latter :
But David was the daring boy
    Who fairly floored *both* Mind and Matter.

    David Hume, both Mind and Matter,
    While he lived, would boldly batter :
      Hume by Will bequeathed to Mill
    His favourite feud with Mind and Matter.

We think we see the Things that be ;
    But Truth is coy, we can't get at her ;
For what we spy is all my eye,
    And isn't really Mind or Matter.

    Hume and Mill on Mind and Matter
    Swear that others merely smatter :
      Sense reveals that Something feels,
    But tells no tale of Mind or Matter.

Against a stone you strike your toe ;
    You feel 'tis sore, it makes a clatter :
But what you feel is all you know
    Of toe, or stone, or Mind, or Matter.

    Mill and Hume of Mind and Matter
    Wouldn't leave a rag or tatter :
      What although we feel the blow ?
    That doesn't show there's Mind or Matter.

We meet and mix with other men ;
  With women, too, who sweetly chatter :
But mayn't we here be duped again,
  And take our thoughts for Mind and Matter ?

> *Sights and sounds like Mind and Matter,*
> *Fairy forms that seem to chatter,*
>   *Are but gleams in Fancy's dreams*
>   *Of Men and Women, Mind and Matter.*

Successive feelings on us seize
  (As thick as falling hail-stones patter) :
The Chance of some return of these,
  Is all we mean by Mind or Matter.

> *Those who talk of Mind and Matter*
> *Just a senseless jargon patter :*
>   *What are We, or you, or he ?—*
>   *Dissolving views, not Mind or Matter.*

We're but a train of visions vain,
  Of thoughts that cheat, and hopes that flatter :
This hour's our own, the past is flown ;
  The rest unknown, like Mind and Matter.

> *Then farewell to Mind and Matter :*
> *To the winds at once we scatter*
>   *Time and Place, and Form and Space,*
>   *And You and Me, and Mind and Matter.*

We banish hence Reid's Common Sense ;
   We laugh at Dugald Stewart's blatter ;
Sir William, too, and Mansel's crew,
   We've done for You, and Mind and Matter.

    Speak no more of Mind and Matter :
    Mill with mud may else bespatter
      All your schools of silly fools,
    That dare believe in Mind or Matter.

But had I skill, like Stuart Mill,
   His own position I could shatter :
The weight of Mill, I count as Nil—
   If Mill has neither Mind nor Matter.

    Mill, when minus *Mind and Matter,*
    Though he make a kind of clatter,
      Must himself just mount the Shelf,
    And there be laid with Mind and Matter.

I'd push my logic further still
   (Though this may have the look of satire) :
I'd prove there's no such man as Mill,—
   If Mill disproves both Mind and Matter.

    If there's neither Mind nor Matter,
    Mill's existence, too, we shatter :
      If you still believe in Mill,
    Believe as well in Mind and Matter.

February 1866.

A FLASK OF ROSY WINE.

A SEMI-SCIENTIFIC SONG.

To make life's pulses gaily go,
Not much too fast, nor yet too slow;
And joy without dejection know, ·
    Were worth a golden mine.
Then try with me the simple art,—
If better views you can't impart,—
To calm the brain and cheer the heart
    With a flask of rosy Wine.

Cognac may better suit with some,
Or Gin and Whisky handier come;
And Glasgow long was fond of Rum
    When merchants met to dine:
But Prudence there her part should play,
The fire with water to allay;
Or take instead, to wet her clay,
    A flask of rosy Wine.

The rustic loves a rousing bout
With home-brewed Ale or bottled Stout :
When these are in the sense is out,
  And wit shows little sign.
For dull and dense *his* thoughts appear
That's drinking and that's thinking beer :
There's nothing keeps the head so clear
  As a flask of rosy Wine.

The Poppy's gifts can pain control,
And waft on wings the ravished soul,
While dreamy visions round us roll,
  Where rainbow-hues combine :
But sad reaction comes at last,
And binds the helpless victim fast :
Such gloomy shadows ne'er o'ercast
  The reign of rosy Wine.

The Hemp,—with which we used to hang
Our prison pets, yon felon gang,—
In Eastern climes produces Bang,
  Esteemed a drug divine.
As Hashish dressed, its magic powers
Can lap us in Elysian bowers ;
But sweeter far our social hours
  O'er a flask of rosy Wine.

The Tartar's steeds, alive or dead,
Their master keep refreshed and fed ;
The steaks they yield, like saddles spread,
    Are cooked beneath his spine :
The milky mothers of his stud,
Outdoing those that chew the cud,
With Koumiss stir his stagnant blood,
    As if with rosy Wine.

The Indian race of famed Peru,
To mash their malt the Chica chew;
And Tonga's tribes the same way brew
    What serves their Royal line.
The Court collects at dawn of day,
And munching sits and spits away:
The Monarch drinks; but, sooth to say,
    It is not rosy Wine !

A Fungus, on Siberia's plain,
The toper's zeal can so sustain,
That he passes the bottle again and again,
    And gets drunk on the filtered brine.
Our liquor is not quite so strong,
And won't so well the war prolong ;
But much the fitter theme for song
    Is our flask of rosy Wine.

Folks up and down will preaching run
That Man should all such influence shun :
They might as well forbid the Sun
    In heaven at noon to shine.
We needs must seek, while here below,
Some kind Nepenthé for our woe;
And what can softer balm bestow
    Than a flask of rosy Wine?

The banquet is not spread in vain,
Nor instincts given to cause us pain ;
Though Reason's hand should hold the rein,
    And taste our joys refine :
And trust me, friends, for temperate use,
Those vine-clad hills their sweets produce,
And Nature's self exalts the juice
    That fills our flask with Wine.

I'M VERY FOND OF WATER.

A NEW TEMPERANCE SONG.

[Adapted from the Platt Deutsch.]

Ἄριστον μὲν ὕδωρ.

I'm very fond of water,
  I drink it noon and night :
Not Rechab's son or daughter
  Had therein more delight.

I breakfast on it daily ;
  And nectar it doth seem,
When once I've mixed it gaily
  With sugar and with cream.
But I forgot to mention
  That in it first I see,
Infused or in suspension,
  Good Mocha or Bohea.

Chorus—I'm very fond of water,
      I drink it noon and night :
    No mother's son or daughter
      Hath therein more delight.

At luncheon, too, I drink it,
  And strength it seems to bring :
When really good, I think it
  A liquor for a king.
But I forgot to mention—
  'Tis best to be sincere—
I use an old invention
  That makes it into Beer.
        Chorus—I'm very fond of water, &c.

I drink it, too, at dinner ;
  I quaff it full and free,
And find, as I'm a sinner,
  It does not disagree.
But I forgot to mention—
  As thus I drink and dine,
To obviate distension,
  I join some Sherry wine.
        Chorus—I'm very fond of water, &c.

And then when dinner's over,
  And business far away,
I feel myself in clover,
  And sip my *eau sucrée.*
But I forgot to mention—
  To give the glass a smack,

I add, with due attention,
  Glenlivet or Cognac.
    Chorus—I'm very fond of water, &c.

At last when evening closes,
  With something nice to eat,
The best of sleeping doses
  In water still I meet.
But I forgot to mention—
  I think it not a sin
To cheer the day's declension,
  By pouring in some Gin.

Chorus—I'm very fond of water :
    It ever must delight
    Each mother's son or daughter—
    When qualified aright.

June 1861.

THE PERMISSIVE BILL.

A NEW SONG.

" PRAY, what is this Permissive Bill,
    That some folks rave about?
I can't, with all my pains and skill,
    It's meaning quite make out."
O ! it's a little simple Bill,
    That seeks to pass *incog.*,
To *permit* ME—to *prevent* YOU—
    From having a glass of grog.
        Yes ! it's a little simple Bill, &c.

If I'm a Quaker sly and dry,
    Or Presbyterian sour ;
And look on all, with jaundiced eye,
    Who love a joyous hour :
O ! here I've my Permissive Bill,
    You naughty boys to flog,
And *permit* ME—to *prevent* YOU—
    From having a glass of grog.
        O ! yes, I have my little Bill, &c.

If I have wealth or means enough
　　To import a pipe of wine;
While You a glass of humbler stuff
　　Must purchase when you dine:
O! then I use my little Bill,
　　While wetting well my prog,
To *permit* ME—to *prevent* YOU—
　　From buying a glass of grog.
　　　　O! yes, I use my little Bill, &c.

If I'm a fogie quite used up,
　　And laid upon the shelf;
Who grudge that You still dine and sup,
　　As I was wont myself:
Then I bring out my pretty Bill,
　　To impose a little clog,
And *permit* ME—to *prevent* YOU—
　　From having a glass of grog.
　　　　Yes, I bring out my pretty Bill, &c.

If You can drink a sober drop,
　　While I the bottle drain;
And as I don't know when to stop,
　　I'm ordered to " abstain : "
O! then I've my Permissive Bill,
　　Since I'm a worthless dog,

To *permit* ME—to *prevent* YOU—
   Enjoying a glass of grog.
      O ! yes, I've my Permissive Bill, &c.

" However well a man behaves,
   Life's pleasures must he lose,
Because a lot of fools or knaves
   Dislike them, or abuse ? "
O ! yes, and soon a bigger Bill,
   Will go the total hog,
And *permit* ME—to *prevent* YOU—
   Having Mirth as well as Grog.

Chorus—O ! yes, a big Permissive Bill,
      Will go the Total Hog,
     And *permit* ME—to *prevent* YOU—
      Having Liberty, Mirth, or Grog.

June 1866.

GASTER, THE FIRST M.A.

"The ruler of this place was one Master Gaster, the first Master of Arts in the world."—RABELAIS.

THERE's a comical fellow that all of us know,
And who always is with us wherever we go;
But our constant companion and guide though he be,
Yet our eyes never saw him, and never will see.
Of science the source, and of Arts the first Master,—
The name of this wonderful fellow is Gaster.

Search history through with attention and skill,
And you'll find him still busy for good or for ill.
With his mischievous doings you early may grapple
In the old and unhappy affair of the Apple.
Though the Serpent's designs chiefly caused that disaster,
The Serpent was greatly assisted by Gaster.

But when Man was then sentenced to trouble and toil,
It was Gaster that taught him to labour the soil—
To dig and to delve, and to plant for his diet;
And he never would let him a moment be quiet.
Despotic and stern, and a rigid taskmaster,
But an excellent friend and instructor, was Gaster.

After living some ages on water and greens,
Gaster found out that bacon ate nicely with beans ;
And he also found out that, to moisten such food,
Something better than water was needful and good.
The Nymph of the Well owned that Bacchus surpassed her,
And gave way to the Grape, as the liquor for Gaster.

Now baking, and brewing, and hunting, and fishing
Arose from what Gaster was wanting or wishing.
The grain in the furrow, the fruit on the tree,
The flocks on the mountain, the herds on the lee,
All acknowledged his sway; never empire was vaster
Than the fertile dominions thus subject to Gaster.

Geometry sprang from the Nile's spreading flood,
Just that Gaster might know where his landmarks had
    stood ;
And Commerce grew busy by land and by sea,
Just that Gaster at home well-provisioned might be.
See ! the camel, the car, the canoe, the three-master,
All speed with their loads on the missions of Gaster.

Then cities were built, with their shops and their houses,
Where in plenty and peace Gaster feasts and carouses ;
And a half of the houses and shops in a town,
If great Gaster were gone, might as well be pulled down :
So splendid and spacious on pier and pilaster
Rise the halls we've erected in honour of Gaster.

But I ought to observe that the changes thus made
For the most part took place with Dame Poverty's aid :
For Gaster and She, you don't need me to mention,
Are the father and mother of every invention.
When the pockets contain not a single piaster,
The wits become sharp in the service of Gaster.

I own we've had bloodshed by Gaster's advice,
And proceedings besides that were not over-nice.
Neither Rob Roy nor Cacus had been such a thief,
Hadn't Gaster been always so partial to beef.
When the Mosstrooper's wife saw he'd soon be a faster,
She served up his spurs at the bidding of Gaster.

Yet if Gaster would stay in his natural state,
His exactions would seldom be grievous or great.
But Luxury comes with suggestions officious,
And Cookery tempts him with dishes delicious,
And the Doctor's called in, with his rhubarb and castor,
To remove the sad ills of poor surfeited Gaster.

O ! close upon frenzy the maladies border
That Gaster begets when he's long out of order.
Like madmen we hurry, in hopes of release,
To Malvern or Homburg, to Gully or Spiess ;
When perhaps the disease would be put to flight faster,
If we just stayed at home and did justice to Gaster.

Try always to suit Gaster's wants to a tittle,
Nor supply his demands with too much or too little.
You will ne'er put a sick man in hearty condition,
If Gaster won't join and assist the physician.
In vain to a wound you'll apply salve or plaster,
If you don't take the pains to conciliate Gaster.

When Beauty puts forth all its glory and grace,
And unites the full splendour of form and of face ;
When each gesture is joyous, each movement is light,
And the glance of the eye is serene and yet bright ;
When the rose-hue of health tints the pure alabaster,—
Let us own that 'tis partly the doing of Gaster.

Nay, ev'n in your noblest possession, the Mind,
Your dependence on Gaster too often you find.
A redundant repast, a rich supper or *soirée,*
Will oppress the *divinæ particulam auræ ;*
While at times, we may see, no professor or pastor
Teaches kindness and charity better than Gaster.

Oft when petty annoyances ruffle the soul,
And the temper defies philosophic control,
The commotion is quelled, and a calm will succeed,
Through the simple device of inhaling the Weed :
Such magical power has the soothing Canaster
To bring balmy content and good-humour to Gaster.

As for me, who thus venture his praise to proclaim,
And adorn his high worth with his classical name,
Let me hope from my patron these verses may bring
Some appropriate boon to assist me to sing;
For it must be confessed that the poor poetaster
Finds always his best inspiration in Gaster.

October 1862.

NOTE.—If Gaster, as Rabelais says, was a Master of Arts, it seems a precedent for Female Graduation; as Gaster in Greek is feminine

GASTER.

(ADAPTED TO MUSIC.)

Air—The Rogue's March.

IN a far distant age
(*Vide* Rabelais' page)
Lived a fellow, of Arts the first Master :
   And if further you seek,
   I can tell you in Greek,
That the name of this fellow was Gaster.
   An ingenious fellow was Gaster,
     Though he caused us a little disaster :
      For if you'll look in
      To our first parents' sin,
It was partly the greed of this Gaster.

   Thence into the world,
   Out of paradise hurled,
Adam found here a rigid taskmaster,
   Who compelled him to work
   Like a Trojan or Turk,
To provide a subsistence for Gaster :
   O ! a terrible fellow was Gaster,
     Whose demands became vaster and vaster :

Man was destined to toil,
And to grub at the soil,
That there might be some grub to give Gaster.

When the infant first thought
How his milk could be brought
From its fountain of fair alabaster,
The nice milking machine
We so often have seen,
Was found out for the service of Gaster.
O ! Science must bend before Gaster,
Who in talent has often surpassed her :
Ere we knew what the cause
Of a Vacuum was,
It was made by a baby for Gaster.

Man, after the flood,
' Took to animal food,
As to which he had been a strict faster :
And strong meat made him long
To have liquor as strong,
So the grape was fermented for Gaster.
'Twas a perilous crisis for Gaster,
Who began after this to live faster ;
But provided he stop
At a moderate drop,
It may prove a good cordial for Gaster.

And still, at this day,
Gaster figures away,
Our adviser, our guide, our schoolmaster;
For the most things we do
Have one object in view—
To provide a good dinner for Gaster.
Trade and Commerce are fostered by Gaster:
The skiff, and the lofty three-master,
Spread abroad their white sail
To each varying gale,
To bring victuals and drink to friend Gaster.

But it makes me quite grave,
To think how we behave,
When we do not our appetites master;
For we eat, and we swill,
Twice as much as our fill,
Till we smother and suffocate Gaster.
Then the Doctor is sent for to Gaster,
Who prescribes for him rhubarb and castor;
And so dose after dose
In and out of us goes,
To redress the distempers of Gaster.

A connection most rare
Bound the Siamese pair,
More completely than Pollux and Castor;

So the body and soul
Can each other control,
And the mind sympathises with Gaster.
A proper attention to Gaster,
Saves many a potion and plaster:
Even Surgeons have found
That they can't heal a wound,
If they don't first propitiate Gaster.

Would you know the Chief Good
Men so much have pursued,
Since the era of old Zoroaster;
'Tis a conscience serene,
Hands and tongue that are clean,
And a healthy condition of Gaster.
Then fill up a bumper to Gaster:
Not forgetting the poor poetaster,
Who has lent you his time
For this doggerel rhyme,
As a small panegyric on Gaster.

A SONG OF PROVERBS.

Air—Push about the jorum.

In ancient days, tradition says,
    When knowledge much was stinted—
When few could teach and fewer preach,
    And books were not yet printed—
What wise men thought, by prudence taught,
    They pithily expounded;
And proverbs sage, from age to age,
    In every mouth abounded.
        O blessings on the men of yore,
            Who wisdom thus augmented,
        And left a store of easy lore
            For human use invented.

Two of a trade, 'twas early said,
    Do very ill agree, sir;
A beggar hates at rich men's gates
    A beggar's face to see, sir.
Yet trades there are, though rather rare,
    Where men are not so jealous;

Two lawyers know the coal to blow,
    Just like a pair of bellows.
        O blessings, &c.

When tinkers try their trade to ply,
    They make more holes than mend, sir;
Set some astride a horse to ride,
    You know their latter end, sir.
Rogues meet their due when out they fall,
    And each the other blames, sir;
The pot should not the kettle call
    Opprobrious sorts of names, sir.
        O blessings, &c.

The man who would Charybdis shun,
    Must make a cautious movement,
Or else he'll into Scylla run—
    Which would be no improvement.
The fish that left the frying-pan,
    On feeling that desire, sir,
Took little by their change of plan,
    When floundering in the fire, sir.
        O blessings, &c.

A man of nous from a glass house
    Will not be throwing stones, sir;
A mountain may bring forth a mouse,
    With many throes and groans, sir.

A friend in need's a friend indeed,
   And prized as such should be, sir;
But summer friends, when summer ends,
   Are off and o'er the sea, sir.
     O blessings, &c.

Sour grapes, we cry, of things too high,
   Which gives our pride relief, sir;
Between two stools the bones of fools
   Are apt to come to grief, sir.
Truth, some folks tell, lies in a well,
   Though why I ne'er could see, sir;
But some opine 'tis found in wine,
   Which better pleases me, sir.
     O blessings, &c.

Your toil and pain will all be vain,
   To try to milk the bull, sir;
If forth you jog to shear the hog,
   You'll get more cry than wool, sir.
'Twould task your hand to sow the sand,
   Or shave a chin that's bare, sir;
You cannot strip a Highland hip
   Of what it does not wear, sir.
     O blessings, &c.

Of proverbs in the common style
   If now you're growing weary,

I'll try again to raise a smile
　　With two by Lord Dundreary.
You cannot brew good Burgundy
　　Out of an old sow's ear, sir;
Nor can you make a silken purse
　　From very sour small beer, sir.
　　　　O blessings, &c.

Now he who listens to my song,
　　And heeds what I indite, sir,
Will seldom very far go wrong,
　　And often will go right, sir.
But whoso hears with idle ears,
　　And is no wiser made, sir,
A fool is he, and still would be,
　　Though in a mortar brayed, sir.
　　　　O blessings, &c.

January 1864.

SONG AT THE SYMPOSIUM ON MAGA.

Air—The Arethusa.

COME, all good friends who stretch so free
Your legs beneath our Ebony,
In loving lays along with me,
   Proclaim the praise of Maga.
She is a creature not too good
For human nature's daily food:
   And her men are.stanch to their favourite haunch,
   On which they fall like an avalanche,
· And fairly floor it, root and branch,
      In the name of mighty Maga.

'Tis sweet to see, when hard at work,
These heroes armed with knife and fork,
While flashes far the frequent cork
   To refresh the thirst of Maga.
Some dozen dishes swept away
Are but the prologue to our play:
   If a haunch can't be found upon English ground,
   Then the best of blackfaced, duly browned,
   Or the faultless form of a well-fed round,
      Must sustain the strength of Maga.

Our banquet, lately spread to view,
Appears to me an emblem true
Of that served up in season due
   To the monthly guests of Maga.
No rival feast can e'er compare
With Maga's mental bill of fare,
   While her table is gay with a French fricassée,
   A currie, casserole, or a cabriolet,*
   Yet solid substance still bears sway
      In the rich repasts of Maga.

How many myriad mouths attend
Till Maga's hand their meat shall send !
What scholars, poets, patriots, bend
   Their eager eyes on Maga !
The knock that speaks a Number come,
Stirs the soldier's heart like the sound of a drum :
   While with pallid cheer, between hope and fear,
   Fair maidens ask, " Pray, does there appear
   Any more this month of Ten Thousand a-Year,
      In the pleasing page of Maga ? "

What fleets of Granton steamers sail,
Each laden with our monthly bale,
Besides that part that goes by rail,
   Of the wondrous works of Maga !

* A convenient name for any dish that has no other name.

O'er all the earth, what scene or soil
Is not found full of Maga's toil?
　　Every varying breeze wafts her over the seas,
　　While insurance at Lloyd's is done with ease
　　At nothing per cent, or what you please,
　　　　On the craft that carries Maga.

Survey mankind with careful view,
From Cochin-China to Peru,
And take a transverse section too;
　　All read and reverence Maga.
Around the poles, beneath the line,
She rules and reigns by right divine;
　　She is thought no sin by Commissioner Lin;
　　And, waiving at once the point of Pin,
　　The Celestial Empire all take in
　　　　The barbarian Mouth of Maga.

But most her page can joy impart
To many a home-sick Scottish heart,
That owns afar the potent art
　　Possessed by mighty Maga.
The exile sees, at her command,
His native mountains round him stand;
　　In vision clear his home is near,
　　And a murmuring streamlet fills his ear;
　　Till now the fast o'erflowing tear
　　　　Dissolves the spell of Maga.

But next let North inspire the strain:
Ye Muses, ope your richest vein!
Though flattery goes against the grain
   With the master-mind of Maga.
Without him all to wreck would run:
A system then without a sun!
   For his eye and soul, with strong control,
   Enlighten all that round him roll,
   And gild and guide the mighty whole,
      That bears the name of Maga.

Then, now before we bid adieu,
We wish, while yet the year is new,
Succeeding seasons, not a few,
   To the noble North and Maga.
May life's best gifts their progress bless!
May their lights—and their shadows—never be less!
   May they lengthen their lease with an endless in-
      crease!
   Or only then depart in peace,
   When frauds shall fail and follies cease,
      Subdued by North and Maga.

February 1841.

HILLI-ONNEE.

[In the year 1841 Lord Palmerston had a celebrated race-horse called Ilione, the pronunciation of whose name became a matter of dispute on the turf. An appeal having been made to his lordship, he replied, to the surprise of some scholars, that it should be pronounced as if written *Hillionnee*. Apparently this view arose from his lordship's having become a convert to the system of accentual pronunciation. The ordinary English mode of pronouncing the name is that indicated by Pitt in his translation of the Eneid, Book I., when he speaks of the sceptre

- "That wont Ilione's fair hand to grace."]

THE Whigs can boast of many a name,
    Great Normanby and Little Johnny;
But far their foremost child of fame
    Is he that owns fleet Hilli-onnee.

'Mong lords and legs a contest rose
    As fierce as e'er we fought with Bonny:
From words it almost came to blows,
    And still the theme was Hilli-onnee.

And some said this, and some said that;
    No want there was of caco-phony:

With short and long, with sharp and flat,
    They sore misnomered Hilli-onnee.

Then one bethought him of a way
    To terminate this acri-mony;
He called as umpire of the fray,
    The lord that owns fleet Hilli-onnee.

His lordship, though a scholar once,
    At this appeal was much *étonné;*
But loath to be esteemed a dunce,
    He searched his books for Hilli-onnee.

No doubt he well remembered yet
    Old Sophocles's *Hanti-gonnee;*
A clearer case he could not get,
    Nor more in point for Hilli-onnee.

But firmer proofs he sought and found;
    The Greeks, disliking mono-tonny,
Had accents to direct the sound,
    And these showed here 'twas Hilli-onnee.

He wrote his answer, brief, yet bright
    With classic wit and keen i-ronny,
And having quashed the Tories quite,
    He taught us all 'twas Hilli-onnee.

O Peel ! your guilt what tongue can tell !
  'Twas nothing less than rank fe-lonny,
To oust a lord who talks so well
  Of heathen Greek and Hilli-onnee.

Had I the might of Pindar's muse
  To sing the praise of Palmer-stonny;
The deathless prince of Syracuse
  Should yield to him and Hilli-onnee.

Pindar, alas ! is in his grave ;
  But this good page of old E-bonny,
For distant days the names shall save
  Of Palmer-ston and Hilli-onnee.

November 1841.

THE THREE R's.

You must own, Mrs Bull, that your family's large,
　　Say, some two or three millions at least ;
And so many small children must prove a great charge,
　　Which of late has been strangely increased.
To their schooling, of course, we must carefully see,
　　Or a slur on us both it will fling ;
But, as all of the lot cannot gentlefolks be,
　　Why, I think, the three R's is the thing.

One lad must be keeping the cow from the corn,
　　Or must wait on the wandering sheep :
Another must double Cape Wrath or Cape Horn—
　　A cabin-boy far on the deep.
As soon as the plumes on their pinions grow strong,
　　From the nest they are sure to take wing ;
So their time with the schoolmaster cannot be long,
　　And 'tis clear the three R's is the thing.

To read well their Bible, to write to a friend,
　　And to cast up a common account,
This is easily taught, and though this were the end,
　　'Tis a boon of no slender amount.

Would they learn Mathematics, or Grammar, or Greek,
  E'en supposing we gave them their swing?
Or would these make them fitter a service to seek?
  No, no; the three R's is the thing.

Would you deck out a daughter in satin and silk,
  Who must work for the bread she's to eat?
Would you send out your maids to the cow-house to milk,
  With fine kid-leather shoes on their feet?
Should your ploughboys, like folks at the playhouse, be
    dressed,
  As if only to dance and to sing?
No! such tawdry attire would but make them a jest:
  So, again, the three R's is the thing.

Then, my dear, there's a matter I've lately observed,
  Makes me sorely our system distrust:
'Tis that some boys are stuffed, while the others are
    starved,
  Which is cruel as well as unjust.
To the general mass, to the average class,
  We should knowledge and nourishment bring:
Give them plain wholesome fare, but let each have a
    share;
  And for *that* the three R's is the thing.

  1862.

LET US ALL BE UNHAPPY ON SUNDAY.

A LYRIC FOR SATURDAY NIGHT.

Air—We bipeds made up of frail clay.

WE zealots, made up of stiff clay,
　　The sour-looking children of sorrow,
While not over jolly to-day,
　　Resolve to be wretched to-morrow.
We can't for a certainty tell
　　What mirth may molest us on Monday;
But, at least, to begin the week well,
　　Let us all be unhappy on Sunday.

That day, the calm season of rest,
　　Shall come to us freezing and frigid;
A gloom all our thoughts shall invest,
　　Such as Calvin would call over-rigid.
With sermons from morning till night,
　　We'll strive to be decent and dreary:
To preachers a praise and delight,
　　Who ne'er think that sermons can weary.

All tradesmen cry up their own wares;
  In this they agree well together:
The Mason by stone and lime swears;
  The Tanner is always for leather.
The Smith still for iron would go;
  The Schoolmaster stands up for teaching;
And the Parson would have you to know,
  There's nothing on earth like his preaching.

The face of kind Nature is fair;
  But our system obscures its effulgence:
How sweet is a breath of fresh air!
  But our rules don't allow the indulgence.
These gardens, their walks and green bowers,
  Might be free to the poor man for one day;
But no, the glad plants and gay flowers,
  Mustn't bloom or smell sweetly on Sunday.

What though a good precept we strain
  Till hateful and hurtful we make it!
What though, in thus pulling the rein,
  We may draw it so tight as to break it!
Abroad we forbid folks to roam,
  For fear they get social or frisky;
But of course they can sit still at home,
  And get dismally drunk upon whisky.

Then, though we can't certainly tell
    How mirth may molest us on Monday;
At least, to begin the week well,
    Let us all be unhappy on Sunday.

THE THREE MODERATORS.

[Written on the almost simultaneous appearance of three exposi-
tions of ecclesiastical views—the Addresses by the Moderators of the
Established and Free Church Assemblies of Scotland, and an Allo-
cution at Rome by the Pope on the state of the Catholic Church.]

Air—Abraham Newland.

WHEN a clerical set
    In Assembly are met,
They are apt to prove angry debaters ;
    So, their wrath to restrain,
    And due calmness maintain,
They have men that are called Moderators.
All Churches should have Moderators,
And should choose them of peaceable *naturs ;*
    Much trouble it saves
    When some oil on the waves
Can be poured by your true Moderators.

But this good class of men,
I'm afraid, now and then,

To their office of peace have proved traitors;
  And too much, on the whole,
  Have kept blowing the coal,
When they ought to have been Moderators.
What a pity that Church Moderators,
Like so many Vesuvian craters,
  Should send forth, in their ire,
  Thunder, fury, and fire
All around these inflamed Moderators.

  I took pains to compare
  The harangues from the chair
Lately made by two Reverend Paters;
  And I read, the same day,
  What the Pope had to say—
For the Popes are just Rome's Moderators.*
The Pope and our two Moderators
· Are surely not three Agitators!
  Yet it's clear that the *first*,
  Who, I hope, is the worst,
Is no model for true Moderators.

  One famous divine,
  In his humorous line,

* The Pope and Cardinals, in their original constitution, may be said to have been simply the Moderator and Presbytery of Rome, the Cardinals being the supposed clergy of the City Churches.

Could not fail to delight all spectators ;
    But some thought to his tongue
    An astringency clung,
Scarcely known to our old Moderators.
The *third* of these same Moderators
I wish may have some imitators :
    For Bisset to me
    Seemed the best of the three,
And comes nearest our true Moderators.

1862.

THE TOURIST'S MATRIMONIAL GUIDE THROUGH SCOTLAND.

A NEW SONG.

Air—Woo'd and married an' a'.

YE tourists, who Scotland would enter,
   The summer or autumn to pass,
I'll tell you how far you may venture
   To flirt with your lad or your lass ;
How close you may come upon marriage,
   Still keeping the wind of the law,
And not, by some foolish miscarriage,
   Get woo'd and married an' a'.

> *Woo'd and married an' a' ;*
> *Married and woo'd an' a' :*
> *And not, by some foolish miscarriage,*
> *Get woo'd and married an' a'.*

This maxim itself might content ye,
   That marriage is made—by consent ;
Provided it's done *de præsenti*,
   And marriage is really what's meant.

Suppose that young Jockey and Jenny
    Say, " We two are husband and wife;"
The witnesses needn't be many—
    They're instantly buckled for life.

> *Woo'd and married an' a' ;*
> *Married and woo'd an' a' :*
> *It isn't with us a hard thing*
> *To get woo'd and married an' a'.*

Suppose the man only has spoken,
    The woman just giving a nod ;
·They're spliced by that very same token
    Till one of them's under the sod.
Though words would be bolder and blunter,
    The want of them isn't a flaw;
For *nutu signisque loquuntur*
    Is good Consistorial Law.

> *Woo'd and married an' a' ;*
> *Married and woo'd an' a' :*
> *A wink is as good as a word*
> *To get woo'd and married an' a'.*

If people are drunk or delirious,
    The marriage of course would be bad ;
Or if they're not sober and serious,
    But acting a play or charade.

It's bad if it's only a cover
　For cloaking a scandal or sin,
And talking a landlady over
　To let the folks lodge in her inn.

Woo'd and married an' a' ;
Married and woo'd an' a' :
It isn't the mere use of words
Makes you woo'd and married an' a'.

You'd better keep clear of love-letters,
　Or write them with caution and care;
For, faith, they may fasten your fetters,
　If wearing a conjugal air.
Unless you're a knowing old stager,
　'Tis here you'll most likely be lost;
As a certain much-talked-about Major
　Had very near found to his cost.

Woo'd and married an' a' ;
Married and woo'd an' a' :
They are perilous things, pen and ink,
To get woo'd and married an' a'.

I ought now to tell the unwary,
　That into the noose they'll be led,
By giving a promise to marry,
　And acting as if they were wed.

But if, when the promise you're plighting,
　To keep it you think you'd be loath,—
Just see that it isn't in writing,
　And then it must come to your oath.

　　Woo'd and married an' a';
　　Married and woo'd an' a':
　　I've shown you a dodge to avoid
　　Being woo'd and married an' a.

A third way of tying the tether,
　Which sometimes may happen to suit,
Is living a good while together,
　And getting a married repute.
But you who are here as a stranger,
　And don't mean to stay with us long,
Are little exposed to that danger;
　So here I may finish my song.

　　Woo'd and married an' a';
　　Married and woo'd an' a':
　　You're taught now to seek or to shun
　　Being woo'd and married an' a'.

DECIMIS INCLUSIS.

"Many lands in Scotland are enjoyed *cum decimis inclusis et nunquam antea separatis.* All our writers agree that such lands are free from the payment of tithes."—*Erskine's Institute.*

Air—Maggie Lauder.

I'VE often wished it were my fate,
   Enriched by Fortune's bounty,
To own a little nice Estate
   In some delightful county;
Where I, perhaps, with some applause,
   Might cultivate the Muses,
And till my lands, and have a clause
   Cum decimis inclusis.

Wherever no such clause appears,
   You're doomed to much vexation;
The Minister, each twenty years,
   Pursues his augmentation.
Like any fiend he grabs your teind,
   Unless the Court refuses,
And all are sold who do not hold
   Cum decimis inclusis.

That strife to tell, would answer well
   This tune of Maggie Lauder,
When half the Bar are waging war
   About the extra cha'der.
But Outram's wit that scene has hit,
   And all so much amuses,
That I refrain, and turn my strain
   To *decimis inclusis.*

'Twould be a dry and dreary theme,
   With nothing ornamental,
To tell you how the Interim scheme
   Adopts the Proven rental;
The Common agent in the suit,
   Objecting where he chooses,
Is glad when he can well dispute
   Your *decimis inclusis.*

A friend of mine had such a grant,
   And did not get it *gratis;*
But when produced, 'twas found to want
   The *nunquam separatis.*
An Heritor with such a flaw
   His whole exemption loses,
And might as well possess, in law,
   No *decimis inclusis.*

Then ere you buy, your titles try,
    For fear they're in disorder :
An Old Church feu 's the thing for you,
    From some Cistercian Order.
Demand a progress stanch and tight,
    For nothing that excuses,
And see your *nunquam antea* 's right,
    As well as your *inclusis.*

Then free from fear and free from strife,
    Your cares and troubles over,
You'll lead a gay and easy life,
    Among your corn and clover.
The whole Teind Court you'll make your sport,
    Which else such awe diffuses,
" Augment away," you'll blithely say,
    " I've *decimis inclusis.*"

THE SHERIFF'S LIFE AT SEA.

BEING PASSAGES IN THE LIFE OF A MARITIME SHERIFF.

Air—The Sailor's Life at Sea.

How gay is the Sheriff's roving life,
   Who from East to West can roam, boys :
How pleasant, with, or without, his wife,
   To sail for his Island home, boys. (*bis*)
        Roaming here,
        Foaming there,
        Merrily, cheerily,
        Readily, steadily ;
Many an hour of mirth and glee
Has the Sheriff's life at sea, my boys.

When the steam is up and the goods are stored,
   And 'tis time to leave the Forth, boys,
The Sheriff gaily steps on board
   And steers away for the North, boys. (*bis*)
        Steering here,
        Veering there,
        Merrily, cheerily,
        Readily, steadily ;

Quite from care and business free
Is the Sheriff's life at sea, my boys.

But the vessel breasts the eastern breeze,
And St Andrews Bay is near, boys;
And the Sheriff tries to look at his ease,
Though he feels a little queer, boys.   (*bis*)
Pitching here,
Twitching there,
Cheerily, wearily,
Ruefully, woefully;
Much inclined to make Dundee
Is the Sheriff now at sea, my boys.

Now the vessel nears to Aberdeen,
And the plot is growing thick, boys:
On dinner bent the rest are seen,
But the Sheriff's fairly sick, boys.   (*bis*)
Cooking here,
Puking there,
Drearily, wearily,
Groaningly, moaningly;
Plain it is he don't agree
With a Sheriff's life at sea, my boys.

Yet afloat once more, when the waves are calm,
He tempts the treacherous main, boys;

And the Sheriff cures the coming qualm
   With a glass of good champagne, boys. (*bis*)
        Quaffing here,
        Laughing there,
        Cheerily, merrily,
        Readily, steadily;
   Quite intent upon a spree,
   Is the Sheriff now at sea, my boys.

But the zephyr soon becomes a gale,
   And the straining vessel groans, boys ;
And the Sheriff's face grows deadly pale,
   As he thinks of Davy Jones, boys. (*bis*)
        Thinking here,
        Sinking there,
        Wearily, drearily,
        Shakingly, quakingly;
   Not from fear or sickness free
   Is the Sheriff now at sea, my boys.

So the Sheriff now must needs resign,
   For his inside's fairly gone, boys :
And he calls for a glass of brandy-wine,
   And to bed with his gaiters on, boys. (*bis*)
        Lying here,
        Dying there,

Drearily, wearily,
Groaningly, moaningly;
Prostrate laid by fate's decree
Seems the Sheriff now at sea, my boys.

But a joyful strain awakes the Muse,
  Which will quite efface the past, boys;
For the Mail-boat brings the joyful news
  That promotion's come at last, boys.   (*bis*)
        Cheering here,
        Jeering there,
        Merrily, cheerily,
        Readily, steadily:
Fear and sickness far may flee,
For the Sheriff quits the sea, my boys.

NOTE.—This song, describing the imaginary voyage of a Scotch
Sheriff to his maritime dominions, was written as a parody on the
song of "The Sailor's Life at Sea," which was one of the lyrics so
delightfully sung by Professor Wilson. Another parody, in a different style, and by a different but certainly not an inferior hand,
appeared in the Magazine under the title of "The Bagman's Life
on Shore," May 1838.

MESSRS BLACKWOOD & SONS

HAVE PUBLISHED—

WORKS OF PROFESSOR WILSON. Edited by his
Son-in-law, PROFESSOR FERRIER. In Twelve Vols., crown 8vo, £2, 8s.

RECREATIONS OF CHRISTOPHER NORTH. By
PROFESSOR WILSON. In Two Vols. New Edition, with Portrait, 8s.

THE NOCTES AMBROSIANÆ. By PROFESSOR WIL-
SON. With Notes and a Glossary. In Four Vols., crown 8vo, 16s.

TALES. By PROFESSOR WILSON. Comprising 'The
Lights and Shadows of Scottish Life;' 'The Trials of Margaret Lynd-
say;' and 'The Foresters.' In One Vol., crown 8vo, 4s., cloth.

ESSAYS, CRITICAL AND IMAGINATIVE. By
PROFESSOR WILSON. Four Vols., crown 8vo, 16s.

TALES FROM 'BLACKWOOD.' Complete in Twelve
Volumes. Bound in cloth, 18s.

LAYS OF THE SCOTTISH CAVALIERS, AND OTHER
POEMS. By W. EDMONDSTOUNE AYTOUN, D.C.L. Nineteenth Edition.
Fcap. 8vo, 7s. 6d.

ILLUSTRATED EDITION OF PROFESSOR AYTOUN'S
LAYS OF THE SCOTTISH CAVALIERS. By Sir J. NOEL
PATON, &c. In small 4to, printed on toned paper, bound in gilt cloth,
21s.

THE BOOK OF BALLADS. Edited by Bon Gaultier.
With numerous Illustrations by Doyle, Leech, and Crowquill.
Ninth Edition. Gilt edges, post 8vo, 8s. 6d.

POEMS AND BALLADS OF GOETHE. Translated
by W. E. Aytoun and Theodore Martin. Second Edition. 6s., cloth.

BOTHWELL: A Poem. By William Edmondstoune
Aytoun, D.C.L. Third Edition. Fcap. 8vo, 7s. 6d.

FIRMILIAN; or, The Student of Badajoz. A Spas-
modic Tragedy. Fcap. 8vo, 5s.

THE BALLADS OF SCOTLAND. Edited by Pro-
fessor Aytoun. Third Edition. Two Vols., fcap. 8vo, 12s.

LIFE OF PROFESSOR AYTOUN. By Theodore
Martin. Crown 8vo, 12s.

THE HISTORY OF SCOTLAND, from Agricola's
Invasion to the Revolution of 1688. By John Hill Burton.
Vols. I. to IV. 8vo, 56s.

THE BOOK - HUNTER. By John Hill Burton.
Second Edition. Crown 8vo, 7s. 6d.

THE SCOT ABROAD, and the Ancient League with
France. By John Hill Burton. Two Vols., crown 8vo, 15s.

William Blackwood & Sons, Edinburgh and London.

www.ingramcontent.com/pod-product-compliance
Lightning Source LLC
Chambersburg PA
CBHW030002030726
47499CB00008B/2864